Unicorn vs. Goblins

Another Phoebe and Her Unicorn Adventure

Dana Simpson

Andrews McMeel Publishing®

a division of Andrews McMeel Universal

INTRODUCTION

CORY: You know what I think? We should write about how we found out about Phoebe and why we love her.

POESY: Wait, how DID we find out about Phoebe?

CORY: Don't you remember? I brought the first book home, but I didn't like the cover, so I stuck it on your shelf and forgot about it and then—

POESY: —One day I took it off the shelf. We read it, and we liked it.

CORY: That's what I remember, too, more or less. I came into your room to shout at you to brush your hair for school, and you were reading this great comic book and laughing. I told you to put it down and brush your hair and came back five minutes later, and you were still reading it and laughing.

POESY: There's too many "and"s in that sentence.

CORY: Then I took it away from you. I read it, and I started laughing, too.

POESY: Nah, my description is totally better.

[Let the record show that here, Poesy asked to re-read some of the strips in this volume and took the laptop away from me. I couldn't get it back until Alice distracted her with guacamole, and I took the computer back.]

POESY: I like the part where Phoebe goes to music camp and Marigold makes a friend.

[At this point, Cory asked Poesy to draw a Phoebe and Marigold, on a rocket-skateboard, playing music.]

POESY: You mean a hoverboard.

pheobe + Marigold = pheobe gold

CORY: It's easy to compare Phoebe to Calvin and Marigold to Hobbes—I did it when I reviewed that first collection ("If Hobbes was a snarky unicorn and Calvin was an awesome little girl"), but Calvin was kind of a creep, especially to little girls. By contrast, Phoebe has a very well-adjusted relationship with the young dudes in her life—and still manages to be funny as heck when they come around.

I love—LOVE—how Dana finesses the way that Phoebe's parents relate to Marigold, too. Calvin's mom and dad rolled their eyes every time Calvin talked with spittle-flecked excitement about his imaginary friend. But Phoebe's parents are cooled out by Marigold's SHIELD OF BORINGNESS, which means that they can react to her as if she were just one of Phoebe's little pals, albeit a pal with a horn, hooves, and magic powers.

But best of all is Marigold. I mean, her last name is HEAVENLY NOSTRILS. Say that aloud with me. HEAVENLY. NOSTRILS. How much fun is that to say?

All the mischief, the pure id and self-centered, delightful sociopathy of youth is evenly divided between Phoebe and Marigold. They're each other's best friends and worst influences.

When *Sesame Street* launched, the show was all kids' jokes. Think of Barney the $#@@{!#* Dinosaur. About as much fun for adults as a fiberglass smoothie. But Jim Henson and the Children's Television Workshop pulled the show and went back to the drawing board, redesigning it so that it had as many adult jokes as kid ones—and so that adults and kids would have a reason to sit and watch together. Whatever value the show had, they reasoned, it would be multiplied if parents and kids shared an experience together, if they had something to talk about after.

The same principle guided the design of Disneyland. Walt Disney was sick of sitting on the sidelines, watching his daughters go around and around the Griffith Park carousel, so he built a theme park full of stuff that kids could bring their grown-ups on. The rest is history.

[Poesy is now singing a Spice Girls song. Where did she learn that?]

There's just enough humor here that sails over kids' heads and lands squarely on their grown-ups to make this an indispensable read for adults, but there's also an infinitude of kid stuff that we both laughed at. I love so many things about this book, but most of all, I love that we read it together.

— Poesy Taylor Doctorow (age 7)
— Cory Doctorow (age 44)
Burbank, California
August 2015

22

26

36

Before I take you home for dinner, we should stop by Dakota's house.

Why?

I have a pamphlet for her.

"So Your Magic Hair Has Begun Thinking For Itself."

This seems weirdly specific.

Where I come from, it is quite standard.

57

87

93

123

128

A DAY IN THE LIFE OF A GOBLIN POSING AS A KID

158

168

Let's Draw Some Supporting Characters

There are more characters than just Phoebe and Marigold! Here's a look at how I draw some of them.

Dakota and Max

Like Phoebe's, Dakota's head is based on a circle.

Headband

Round little nose

Three eyelash lines... also, her eyes are seldom open all the way

Hair is mostly curly lines

Max's is more of an oval.

Eyes are dots in his glasses

Wedge nose

Max's glasses have changed since the previous book! (He got new ones)

Both of them are a little taller and skinnier than Phoebe.

Hand on hip— she's always kind of striking a pose

Dakota's body is also based on circles

Max's body is based on an oval, like his head

Seldom looks up from his phone!

Always wears black

Todd the Candy-Breathing Dragon

No pupils

Curly horns

Pointy beak face

Head and body based on circles (they're SO useful)

Dragon wings are a "hand" shape—I recommend practice

Todd is very small— here's Phoebe's hand for reference

His tail (and horns) are striped like a candy cane

Florence Unfortunate Nostrils

Florence looks a lot like her sister Marigold Heavenly Nostrils in some ways, but there are also some big differences.

Her mane (and some of her tail) are wavy lines

Her glasses hook behind her ears

Always spiders, with Florence

Her nose is less pointy than Marigold's, and her nostrils are bigger

Florence is shorter than her sister, and the difference is mostly legs

Goblins

Your typical goblin

Queen Prunella Von Bläart

mohawk

Goblin heads are possibly the roundest

ragged-edged ears

slit pupils, like a cat

nostrils, but no real nose

fangs

their bodies are sort of pear-shaped, which is really two different-sized circles

Short, kind of bent legs

floppy hair

she has a unique eye shape, (but they all have big mouths)

The queen gets to have ornamentation

Goblins come in different heights, shapes, spot patterns...they probably vary as much as humans.

Questing Mix

Marigold might be able to survive on grass when she and Phoebe go on their quest to save Dakota from the goblins, but Phoebe will need something to snack on, and you will too! This special trail mix is easy to take along or to share with friends.

INGREDIENTS:

½ cup peanuts or other nuts

½ cup mini pretzels or 1-inch pieces small pretzels

½ cup semisweet chocolate chips

½ cup dried cranberries or cherries

¼ cup Goldfish crackers

¼ cup raisins

¼ cup sunflower seeds

INSTRUCTIONS:

In a large bowl, combine all the ingredients and toss to mix well.

The trail mix will keep in an airtight container at room temperature for at least 2 weeks.

Makes about 8 servings, about 3 cups.

Alice and the Unicorn

Not surprisingly, the unicorn makes an appearance in the works of Lewis Carroll, creator of the most delightful whimsy of the Victorian age. In *Through the Looking Glass and What Alice Found There*, Alice encounters a unicorn in a passage that captures the essential paradox of the legendary beast:

> ". . . He was going on, when his eye happened to fall upon Alice: he turned round instantly, and stood for some time looking at her with an air of the deepest disgust.
>
> 'What—is—this?' he said at last.
>
> 'This is a child!' Haigha replied eagerly . . . 'We only found it today. It's as large as life, and twice as natural!'
>
> 'I always thought they were fabulous monsters!' said the Unicorn. 'Is it alive?"
>
> 'It can talk,' said Haigha solemnly.
>
> The Unicorn looked dreamily to Alice, and said, 'Talk, child.'
>
> Alice could not help her lips curling into a smile as she began: 'Do you know, I always thought Unicorns were fabulous monsters, too? I never saw one alive before!'
>
> 'Well, now we *have* seen each other,' said the Unicorn, 'if you'll believe in me, I'll believe in you. Is that a bargain?'"

Andrews McMeel Publishing
a division of Andrews McMeel Universal
1130 Walnut Street, Kansas City, Missouri 64106

www.andrewsmcmeel.com

ISBN: 978-1-4494-8020-2

Library of Congress Control Number: 2015954011

ATTENTION: SCHOOLS AND BUSINESSES

Andrews McMeel books are available at quantity discounts with bulk purchase for educational, business, or sales promotional use. For information, please e-mail the Andrews McMeel Publishing Special Sales Department:
specialsales@amuniversal.com.

Check out these and other books at ampkids.com

Also available:
Teaching and activity guides for each title.
AMP! Comics for Kids books make reading FUN!